For Jeffy (a.k.a. The Beast of Glenisla) – the most dangerous pet of all – LH

For Milo Mantle, my very own fiery (but loveable) dragon – AM

BLOOMSBURY CHILDREN'S BOOKS
Bloomsbury Publishing Plc
50 Bedford Square, London, WC1B 3DP, UK
Bloomsbury Publishing Ireland Limited
29 Earlsfort Terrace, Dublin 2, Ireland

BLOOMSBURY, BLOOMSBURY CHILDREN'S BOOKS
and the Diana logo are trademarks of Bloomsbury Publishing Plc

First published in Great Britain 2025 by Bloomsbury Publishing Plc

Text copyright © Lindsay Hirst 2025
Illustrations copyright © Alice McKinley 2025

Lindsay Hirst and Alice McKinley have asserted their rights under the Copyright,
Designs and Patents Act, 1988, to be identified as the Author and Illustrator of this work

A catalogue record for this book is available from the British Library

ISBN 978 1 5266 6715 1 (HB)
ISBN 978 1 5266 6713 7 (PB)
ISBN 978 1 5266 6714 4 (eBook)

1 3 5 7 9 10 8 6 4 2

Printed and bound in China by Leo Paper Products, Heshan, Guangdong

FSC
MIX
Paper | Supporting
responsible forestry
FSC® C020056
www.fsc.org

To find out more about our authors and books visit www.bloomsbury.com and sign up for our newsletters

For product safety related questions contact productsafety@bloomsbury.com

The DANGEROUS Pet Lover's Guide to DRAGONS

Lindsay Hirst

BLOOMSBURY
CHILDREN'S BOOKS
LONDON OXFORD NEW YORK NEW DELHI SYDNEY

Alice McKinley

Hello, brave reader, and welcome
to the best (and only)

Guide to Dangerous Pets.

The information you'll find here will be
everything you need to know about looking
after your **terrifying** beast.

Of all the dangerous pets in the world,
you've chosen THE most ferocious of all.

Yes . . .

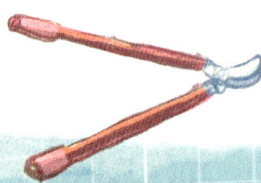
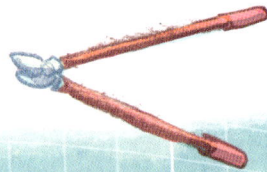

Exhib. 1
Egg

LIBRARY CARD

TITLE:

AUTHOR:

DATE | NAME

THE DRAGON

Dragons are well known for being sulky and difficult. However, by following these simple but important guidelines, you might just be able to create a lovable and (almost) friendly pet.

FINDING YOUR DRAGON

There are many ways to acquire a dragon – some more dangerous than others.

So, think carefully about how and where to find yours.

TOO MEAN! ✗

TOO COLD ✗

SWAMP DRAGONS ✓ YES!

EGGS FOR
ADOPTION

Also, PLEASE adopt them when they're young. The grown-up ones are extremely grumpy (and farty).

NOTE: BABY DRAGONS ALSO FART BUT THE SMELL IS MUCH NICER

HOUSING YOUR DRAGON

All dragon breeds are different.

There are **BIG** ones . . .

and small ones.

Mild ones . . .

and **wild** ones.

Choose one that will fit in well
and not annoy the neighbours too much.

NOTE:
THE BIG WILD ONES
ARE PERFECT
IF YOU LIVE
ALONE IN THE
MOUNTAINS
OR ON A DESERTED
ISLAND →

Bonding With Your New Buddy

If you're very lucky, it'll be **love** at first sight.

However, for most people, bonding with a dragon takes time and hard work.

Try to find out about your pet's likes and dislikes . . .

and remember to ALWAYS stay calm and friendly.

NOTE:
IT'S A GOOD
IDEA TO
HAVE A FIRE
EXTINGUISHER
HANDY AT ALL
TIMES

FIRE
B'
GONE

Do NOT upset your dragon.

FEEDING

Dragons love hunting, so try to make mealtimes fun
by hiding their food in **unusual** places.

They're particularly fond of meat, so ask
the local butcher to make regular deliveries.

This will prevent any **unwanted** behaviour.

DEALING WITH DIFFICULT HABITS

Dragons have lots of difficult habits but the most troublesome are:

collecting shiny things . . . and breathing fire.

Not being allowed to have a shiny thing   =   angry dragon   =   breathing fire

So, very simply, do NOT anger your dragon. Hide all your shiny things, and only give them to your pet as a reward for good behaviour.

Dragons **love** to hoard their treasure,
so give them space to make a lair.
Doing this will make them feel
happy and calm.

NOTE:
NEVER, UNDER ANY
CIRCUMSTANCE, TAKE
ANY OF THE ITEMS
BACK. IT WILL
NOT
GO WELL!

GROOMING AND WASHING YOUR DRAGON

Dragons don't like water so, whatever you do . . .

DON'T try to wash them.

I repeat, DON'T try to wash them.

PLAYTIME

Once you've bonded with your dragon, it's time to play some simple games.

Their favourite game is hide-and-seek. (They love to seek).

Dragons can be VERY sore losers so,
unless you're feeling brave,
remember to let them win!

NOTE: PLEASE DON'T EVER SNEAK UP ON A DRAGON WHEN YOU'RE NOT PLAYING A GAME. (SEE DEALING WITH DIFFICULT HABITS)

Dragons have **wings** . . . so they can (and will) fly away at any moment.

This is good exercise for them.

Some won't go far, and will come back when called,
but others might be more adventurous.

It's a sad and lonely time when your dragon doesn't return . . .
but **try** not to worry.

You might want to put some posters up . . .

HAVE YOU SEEN MY DRAGON?

LOST

or contact The Dangerous Pets Lost and Found Department.

HAVE YOU SEEN MY INVISIBLE FRIEND?

ESCAPED! PET CENTAUR

MISSING IN THE MOUNTAINS

LOST AT SEA

WANTED £££

CLIP CLOP CLIP CLOP

NEIGHTHAN

LOST AND FOUND

HU-MANE RESOURCES

But, apart from that,
you'll just have to wait . . .

and wait.

And IF you've followed these very important
guidelines, then one day . . .

. . . you'll probably find that your best buddy will come home again

because they've really, **really** missed you.

NOTE:
YOUR DRAGON MIGHT
NOT BE ALONE, SO
PLEASE
BE PREPARED

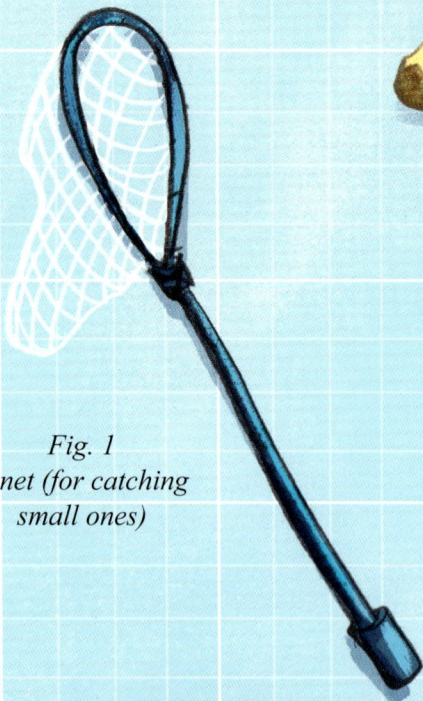

Fig. 1
A net (for catching
small ones)

Fig. 2
A tempting snack

Fig. 3
For spotting

Fig. 8
A rope

Fig. 9
A gift

Fig. 7
Extinguisher.
(You know . . .
because of the
flames.)

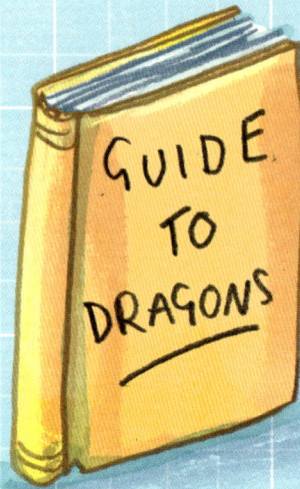

FIRE
B'
GONE

GUIDE
TO
DRAGONS

Fig. 12
The Book

Fig. 15
A shiny thing

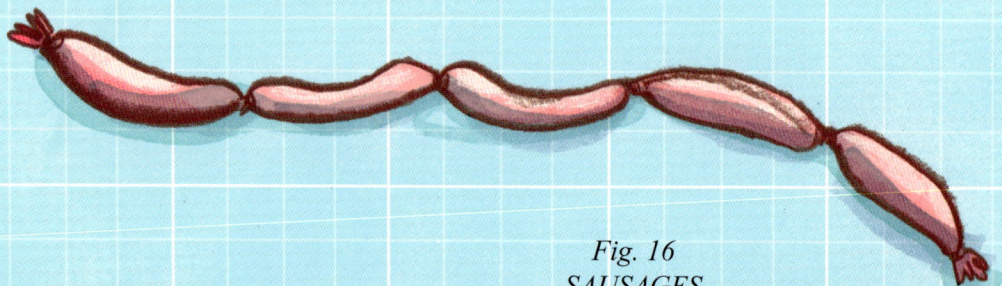

Fig. 16
SAUSAGES

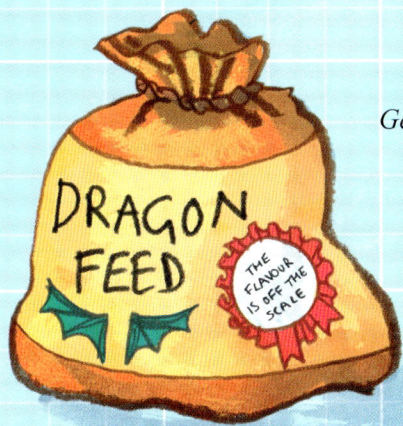
Fig. 4
Get one bag (or 20)

Fig. 5
Some fun literature

Fig. 6
Mr Tiddles

Fig. 10
Extra wings
to wear

Fig. 11
A rucksack

Fig. 13
A disguise (just
in case)

Fig. 14
A gnome (they
like gnomes)

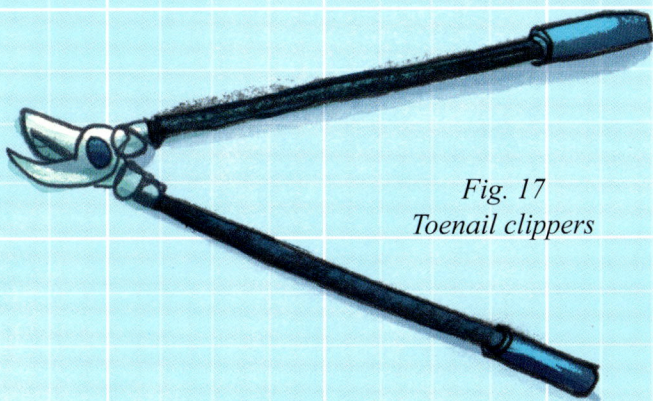
Fig. 17
Toenail clippers

Fig. 18
Lost and found
posters

For more information about
dealing with dragon families,
please see:

The Dangerous
Pet Lover's Guide to
Surviving a Beastly Brood